Have You Ever Seen a Bear with a Purple Smile?

Written By Laura Budds

Illustrated by Kadie Zimmerman

FARCOUNTRY PRESS

ISBN: 978-1-59152-114-3

Previously published by Laura Budds / As Big As The Sky Publishing
through Sweetgrass Books, an imprint of Farcountry Press.

FARCOUNTRY
PRESS

For more information about our books, write Farcountry Press,
P.O. Box 5630, Helena, MT 59604; call (800) 821-3874;
or visit www.farcountrypress.com.

Production date: February 2022
Plant name: Shenzhen Decentmate Printing Co., Ltd.
Plant location: Shenzhen, China
Batch number: 220190

Printed in China.

26   25   24   23   22   6   7   8   9   10

To my children Thomas and Olivia

from whom I get my strength and joy each and everyday.

**Mommy, have you ever seen
a bear with a purple smile?**

How does a bear
get a purple smile?

By eating huckleberries
that grow in the wild.

Huckleberries sound yummy—
Do they taste
sour or sweet?

Ooh, so sweet!
So much so they tickle your nose
all the way down to your toes.

Where are the bears
with the purple smiles?

They're in the woods,
walking mile after mile
searching for the next
huckleberry pile.

We'd like to see a
bear with a purple smile.
Let's look for one!

Ooh no, not now. Huckleberry season is all done.
But, when the snow melts and the flowers bloom,
you can bet bears with purple smiles will be out soon.

So, when you find a huckleberry patch,
Be on the lookout and you just might catch...

...a bear with a purple smile.

ABOUT THE AUTHOR:

Laura Budds is a mother of two young children. Originally from California, she moved to Missoula, Montana, in 1997 searching for the great outdoors. Laura enjoys spending time with her family doing everyday Montana activities such as hiking, camping, and boating. Her love for children's books comes from many years of reading to her two children. Rhyming picture books are her favorite.

ABOUT THE ILLUSTRATOR:

Kadie Zimmerman was born and raised in Kalispell, Montana, close to Flathead Lake and Glacier National Park. She studied at the University of Montana and graduated with a degree in art. Kadie had a passion for art from a very young age and still loves to draw pictures of animals and dinosaurs. She loves to learn and explore Montana's beautiful outdoors.

PHOTO COURTESY OF ERIC JESCHKE

Huckleberry season is short and varies from summer to summer. It usually starts late July to early August. They are found in higher elevations and if you were to find a good huckleberry patch that is a secret not to share with many. The competition is fierce and not just among humans; you may come across grizzlies that find huckleberries to be a favorite treat. When picked and brought home they can be made into the best jams, jellies, barbeque sauces, syrups, and ice cream. The taste is similar to blueberries but much sweeter.